THE PATCHWORK BIKE

For Mali and Maya
For Jude and Gracie
M. B. C.

For Loyola and Manolo
V. T. R.

First U.S. edition 2018

First published in Australia and New Zealand
in 2016 by Hachette Australia.

Library of Congress Catalog Card Number pending
ISBN 978-1-5362-0031-7

18 19 20 21 22 23 CCP 10 9 8 7 6 5 4 3 2 1

Printed in Shenzhen, Guangdong, China

This book was typeset in Sweeper.
The illustrations were done in acrylic on recycled cardboard.

Candlewick Press
99 Dover Street
Somerville, Massachusetts 02144

visit us at www.candlewick.com

THE PATCHWORK BIKE

MAXINE BENEBA CLARKE   illustrated by **Van Thanh Rudd**

CANDLEWICK PRESS

This is the village where we live
inside our mud-for-walls home.

These are my **crazy** brothers,

and this is our fed-up mum.

Here is the sand hill
we built to slide down,

whooping

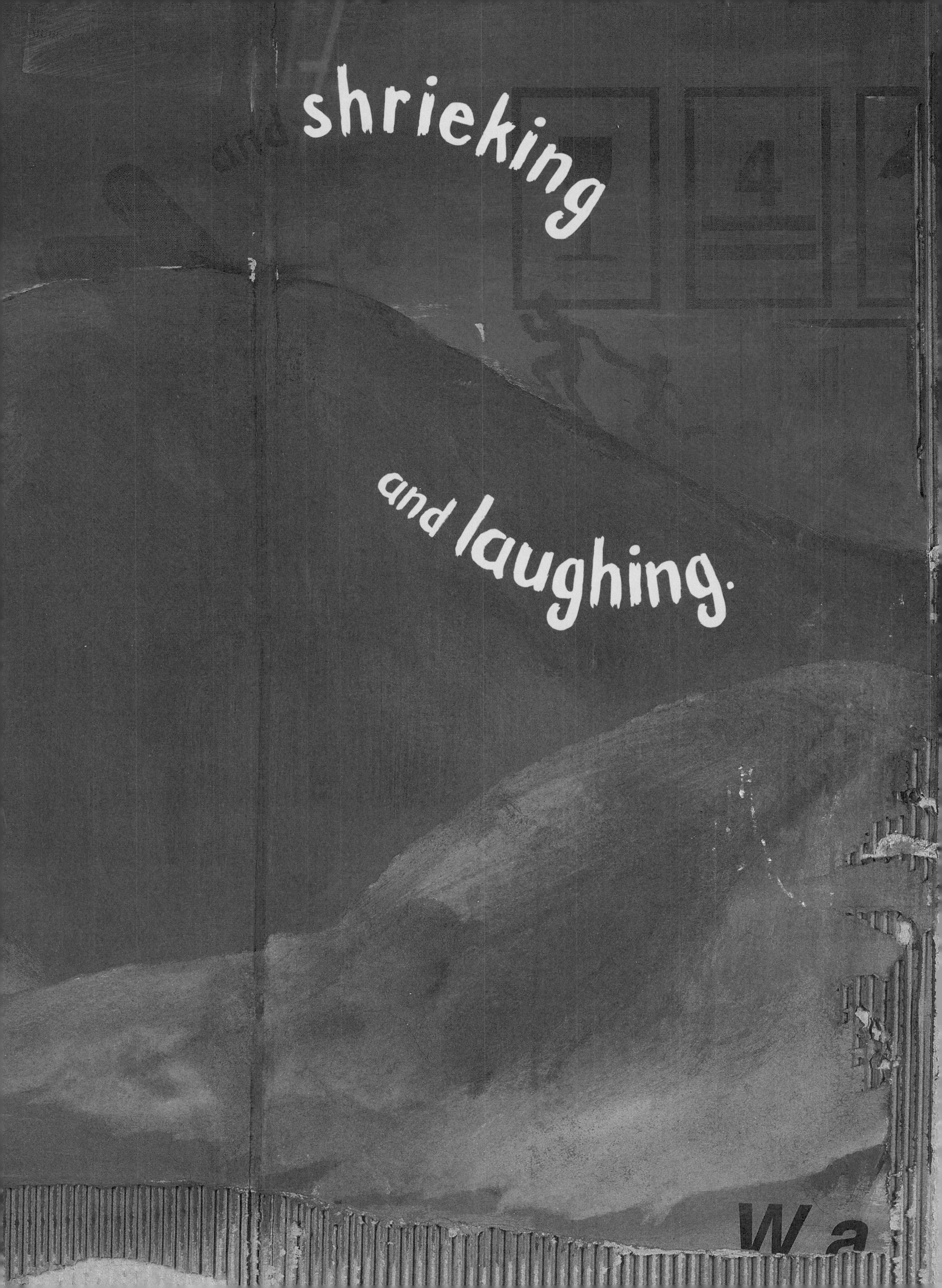

shrieking

and laughing.

This is the big Fiori tree
where we go jumping and climbing.

out in the no-go desert,
under the stretching-out sky.

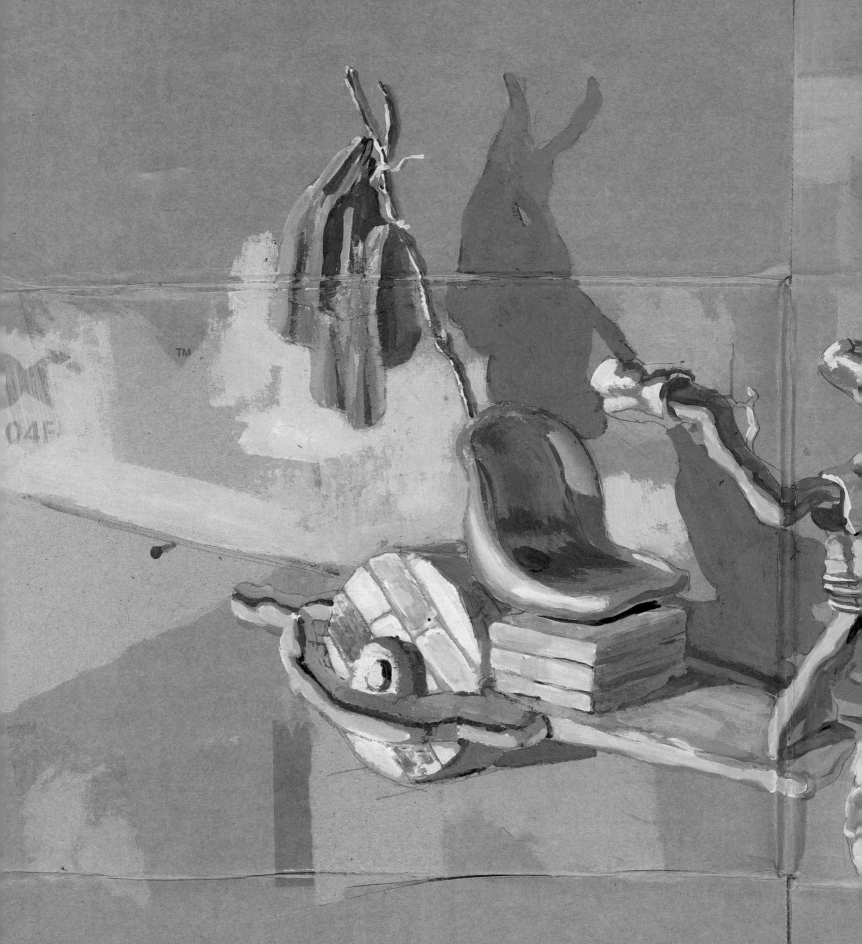

But the **best** thing of all
in our village

is me and my brothers' bike.

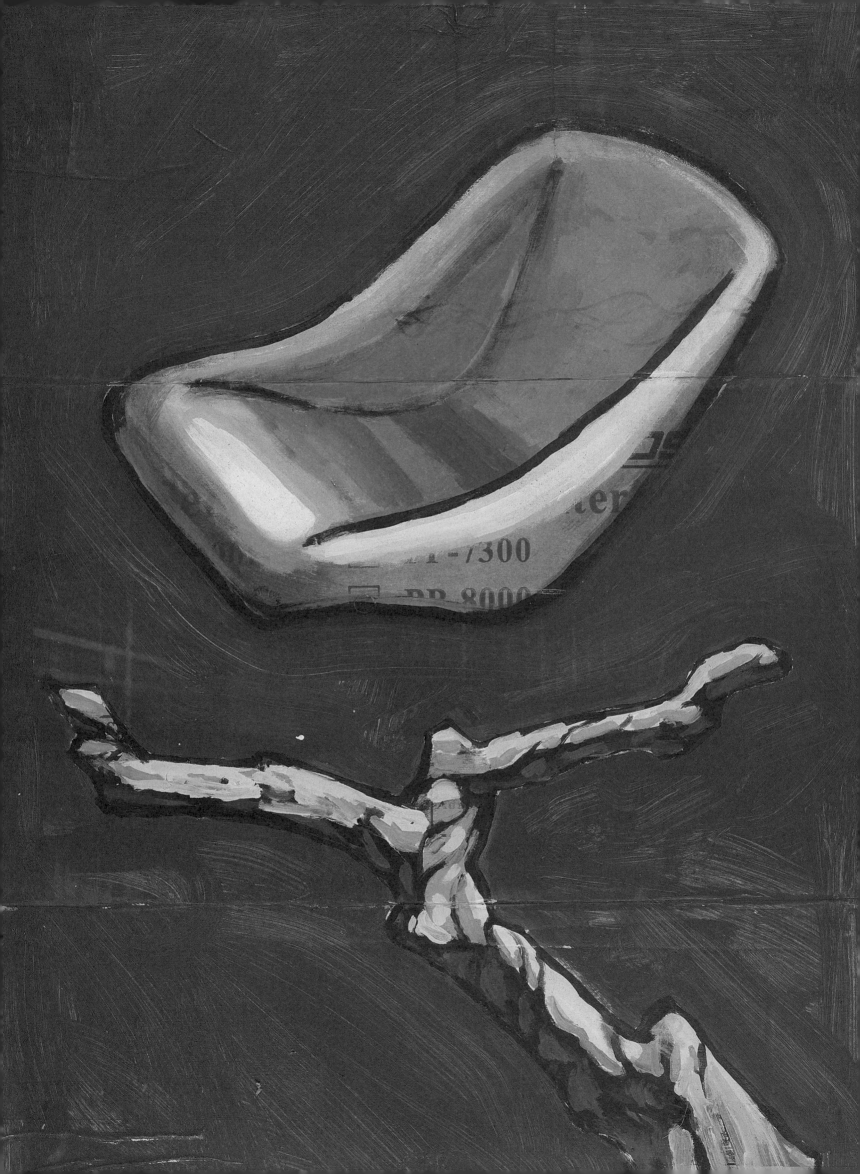

It has a bent bucket seat
and handlebar branches

that **shicketty shake**
when we ride over sand hills.

It has bashed tin-can handles
and wood-cut wheels

that **winketty wonk**
when we speed through the fields.

It has a flag that's made
from a flour sack

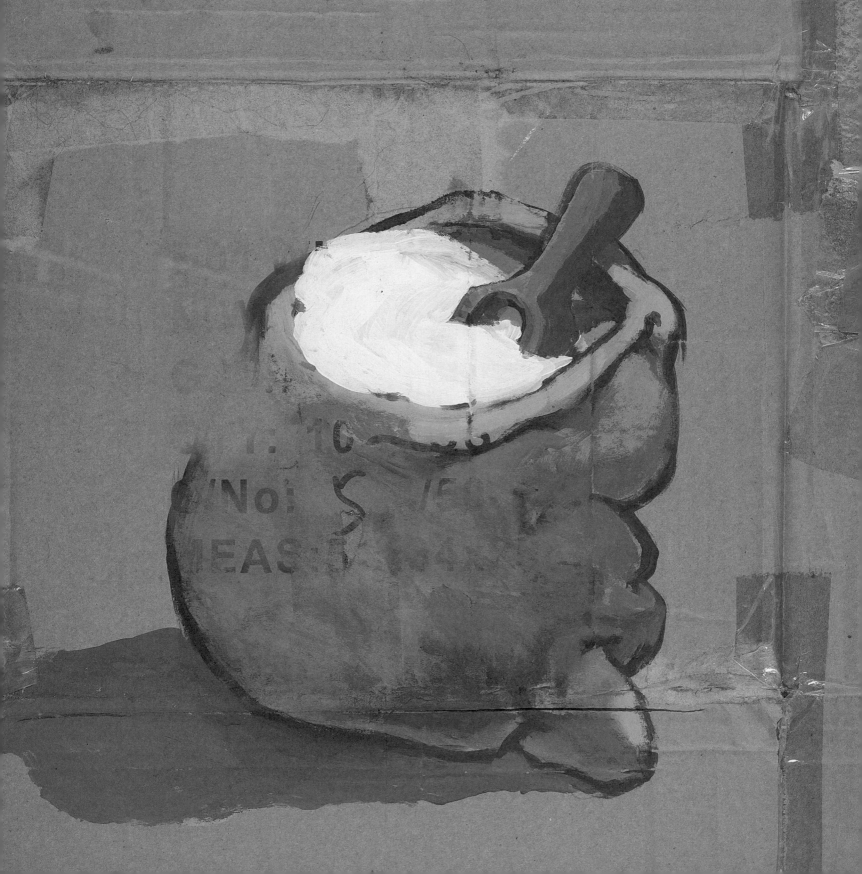

and a bell that used to be Mum's milk pot.

It has painted-on lights
and a bark license plate

that keeps falling off,
so we have to remake it.

It can **bumpetty bump**
through the village,

glide right through
our mud-for-walls home,

carrying me and both of my brothers
right past our fed-up mum.

The best thing of all to play with
under the **stretching-out sky**

at the edge of the
no-go desert . . .

is me and my brothers' bike.

A NOTE ABOUT *THE PATCHWORK BIKE* FROM MAXINE BENEBA CLARKE

The inspiration for *The Patchwork Bike* came from a piece in my short story collection *Foreign Soil*. The story, "David," takes place alternately in Australia and on the African continent and features a child who has a bike made out of scrap findings. Most kids have a bike, have seen a bike, or have longed for a bike. The woman in the story "David" is a Muslim mother, and I was thrilled when I saw Van's rendering of her—that painting in particular is really stunning and beautiful. A mother sent me a message written by her son after the book won a Children's Book Council of Australia award, and the letter said, "Thank you for your book. I'm glad your book won a prize. The mum in your book looks like my mum."

Poverty is in some ways universal, though the landscape of the book is third-world poverty. I hope this book gets into schools and libraries so that kids from all socioeconomic backgrounds can have access to it. I've had times in my life when I've lived close to the poverty line with small children. What these times taught me was how to make something out of nothing, and that children will try to find joy no matter the circumstances. Dire circumstances can be imposed, and can be or seem debilitating, and imagination is really important—both in terms of play and in terms of being able to imagine yourself out of poverty and look for a better future. It was really important to me to try to convey that as a message. The girl and boys in the story love their patchwork bike just as much as a kid with a brand-new, expensive BMX bike might love theirs—or maybe even more. All they see in it is possibility and fun.

A NOTE ABOUT THE ILLUSTRATIONS FROM VAN THANH RUDD

Maxine allowed me a lot of freedom to explore the imagery for *The Patchwork Bike*. I imagined the narrator of the story as a young girl and saw her "brothers" as symbols of the connection between the African and North American continents, with the cop car representing an oppressive economic system hundreds of years old. One of the brothers atop the cop car with hands up in the air is reminiscent of the "don't shoot" element of the Black Lives Matter protests, and the other brother in a ballet-like move is inspired by the Occupy Wall Street poster (2011) showing a ballerina atop the Wall Street bull statue. I enthusiastically mentioned this creative development to Maxine and she loved it. So it seemed the word "crazy" was taking on a whole new complexion—verging on sanity perhaps. I have been detained, harassed, and racially profiled by police for my activism and art, so I understood quite early the dubious role of the cops.

Much of my art has been centered on fighting against the many forms of oppression and exploitation that this global economic system cultivates, so I was really excited when the BLM movement rose up. Like the Arab Spring and the Occupy movements, I find inspiration in how we can unite and fight back. To me, the kids painting "BLM" on a bark license plate was their way of showing pride in what they had created out of limited resources and also linking themselves to a long history of rebellion.